Fancy Nancy
in Disguise

Fancy Nancy in Disguise

Ruth Craft

illustrated by Nicola Smee

COLLINS

William Collins Sons & Co Ltd
London · Glasgow · Sydney · Auckland
Toronto · Johannesburg

First published 1988
© text Ruth Craft 1988
© illustrations Nicola Smee 1988

British Library Cataloguing in Publication Data
Craft, Ruth
Fancy Nancy in disguise
I. Title   II. Smee, Nicola
813′.54 [J]

ISBN 0-00-184249-8

Typeset by Columns of Reading
Printed and bound in Great Britain
by Billings and Sons Ltd, Worcester

Contents

for Jane Fior

1
Fancy Nancy in Disguise

Fancy Nancy was five years old and she lived with her mother and her father and her baby brother, Thomas. Fancy Nancy called Thomas – Smelly Baby – because most of the time he was a bit smelly. The only time he smelled clean, fresh and lovely was after he'd had his bath in the evenings. The rest of the time he smelled of old food, old drinks and old nappies. Thomas could walk but he preferred to crawl. He could crawl very fast. The skin on his knees was quite rough and hard.

One Saturday lunchtime, Fancy Nancy's father said he might go along to the Jumble Sale in the church hall. He was going to take Thomas and would Fancy Nancy like to come too?

"Or you could stay and help me," said

her mother. "I'm going to put up the new tiles in the bathroom."

Fancy Nancy thought hard. She liked helping with jobs like putting up tiles because it was fun pushing the tiles into the soft, splodgy cement. But on the other hand, Jumble Sales were useful places. The trainers that Fancy Nancy was wearing at the moment came from a Jumble Sale. They had a tiger's head printed on the back of the heels.

She decided to go to the Jumble Sale.

"Keep an eye on Thomas," said Fancy Nancy's mother. "Remember when we went to the Jumble Sale at school and he escaped and fell into the Lucky Dip!"

"Nobody would be very lucky if they fished out Smelly Baby!" said Fancy Nancy.

The Jumble Sale had only just started when they all arrived. There were long queues of people pushing their way towards the stalls. Fancy Nancy couldn't see any of the things that were for sale because there were so many people in front of her, including a very big lady in a fluffy red coat. Fancy Nancy was just in time to stop Smelly Baby from grabbing a handful of coat and putting it in his mouth.

At last they got to the stalls and Fancy Nancy's father gave her 50p to spend and said he was going over to buy some raffle tickets and look for some home-made jam. Fancy Nancy looked at the stall. There were jerseys and boots, bangles and jam jars, a lawnmower, some records, buttons and old cocoa tins, socks and mittens, long evening trousers and short party dresses, hats, a hat stand, lots of belts, a box of buckles and two footballs. And that was just one stall. There was a stall for home-made cakes, another for old books, magazines and comics, a Tombola and lots of prizes to be raffled. Fancy Nancy could see her father and Smelly Baby buying the home-made jam.

She rummaged through a pile of navy jumpers and black socks. They were very ordinary and not interesting at all but tangled up in them was a shopping basket that had bright red and blue whales sewn all over it. Fancy Nancy liked whales so she grabbed at one handle of the basket. The very big lady in the fluffy red coat grabbed the other side of the basket at the same time and pulled. But Fancy Nancy pulled just a little bit harder and the bag came away free in her hand.

"How much is this?" she asked the woman behind the stall.

"Ten pence to you, love," said the woman.

Fancy Nancy handed over her 50p and put her change away safely in her pocket. And then she saw the dress.

It was a grown up's dress and it was long and swishy and emerald green. The dress was covered in flowers made from sparkly and glittering sequins. It was hanging on a hanger on a rail and Fancy Nancy could see that there was a tear across the hem and that the big floppy bow around the middle of the dress had come loose.

"Jumping Jingles!" said Fancy Nancy to herself. "That dress is just what I need for my next disguise!" Fancy Nancy already had one disguise, made out of a big black hat, a black blazer and a pair of sun-glasses. But she had used it so many times that everybody knew it was Fancy Nancy underneath. If she dressed up in the green dress – especially if she could get it home from the Jumble Sale without her father or Smelly Baby seeing it – then she would be able to surprise everybody.

"I'll get it wrapped up in paper and squeeze it down tight in the bottom of my whale basket," she said to herself.

The dress cost exactly 40p but Fancy Nancy didn't mind spending all her money.

Her father was a little surprised that she seemed to have spent all her money on an old shopping basket, but *he* didn't see the brown paper parcel tucked in the bottom of it.

Fancy Nancy's father had bought a useful garden trowel, a box of electric plugs and a blue jersey which Fancy Nancy thought was quite smart – if a bit plain. She chattered away to her father about all the things *he'd* bought so that he wouldn't be thinking too much about what *she'd* bought. Smelly Baby ate an apple as he rode along in his push-chair. Someone had given it to him as a bribe to stop him poking the big basket of fruit which was first prize in the raffle. He was too busy chewing to be interested in Fancy Nancy's basket.

When they got home, Fancy Nancy very quickly showed her mother her basket and then ran upstairs with it to her room. She shut the door tight and looked around for somewhere to hide the green dress. She looked at the bunk beds. She slept in the bottom bunk but she thought that if she

climbed up to the top bunk and put the
green dress under the pillow it would be
safe.

When the dress was safely hidden,
Fancy Nancy went downstairs for her
supper with her plan for action buzzing
round in her head. She was going to
surprise her mother and father with her

new disguise later on that evening after they thought she was tucked up in bed asleep. So she was in rather a hurry to get bed-time over and done with. She gobbled down her supper, splashed through her bath, swished through her teeth and said she didn't want a story tonight – she was too tired. Then she raced upstairs to her room, turned off the light, jumped into bed, shut her eyes tight and was breathing heavily by the time her mother and father came to say, "Good night."

Fancy Nancy heard her mother say, "Poor little thing! She's exhausted!"

"Mmmnn!" said her father. "I'm not so sure!"

After a while, Fancy Nancy could hear the television downstairs which meant that her mother and father were safely watching the Saturday night film. She crept out of bed and brought down the green dress from the top bunk. She slipped it on over her pyjamas and found a pair of high-heeled shoes from her dressing-up box. When she put them on, the dress wasn't quite so long and floppy around her feet. She rummaged through the dressing-up box to find a hat that would cover her face. There was a black beret that she could pull down over her nose or a floppy straw hat with a big brim and a rose

pinned to it. She chose the floppy hat and pulled the brim hard down over her face. She found her spy's bag (which was an old black shoulder bag), and made sure she had all her spying equipment ready. There was a magnifying glass, a small pair of binoculars from a Christmas cracker and a bottle of deadly poison made from red food colouring, salt, mustard and scrunched-up leaves from the hedge.

Carefully and quietly, Fancy Nancy left her room and crept downstairs. *Very* carefully and quietly she tip-toed along to the living room and opened the door.

Her mother and father were sitting in their armchairs watching the film and *they didn't even notice her.* She got down on her knees and crawled quietly around the room looking at the floor and the skirting boards with her magnifying glass, hunting for clues. She could tell Smelly Baby had been crawling around there. There were sticky finger marks all along the edge of the boards and an old half-chewed top of a cereal packet was lying on the floor in one corner. It was all grey and squidgy.

Suddenly her mother leapt out of her chair and screamed! She had just seen a strange creature in a bright green evening dress, high-heeled shoes and a floppy hat crawling along the living room floor with a magnifying glass!

Her father stood up and yelled, "Who are you? What's going on?"

Fancy Nancy got to her feet and pulled the brim of the hat even further over her face. She said in a deep, growly voice, "I am Elizabeth Louella and I am here to spy

on witches, bad wizards and trolls and to destroy them with my deadly poison!"

And she took the deadly poison out of her spy's bag and shook the bottle so that the liquid glowed red.

Fancy Nancy's mother and father breathed a sigh of relief. "I see," said her father. "Well I don't think there are any witches or wizards or trolls in here. There might be some in the kitchen!" he said hopefully, looking as if he would like to settle down and watch the film again.

Fancy Nancy thought about that for a minute and decided she didn't want to go into the empty kitchen looking for witches, trolls and wizards. She pulled her hat off.

"Did you know it was me?" she asked her mother and father.

"Well, to be honest. . ." said her mother, "I didn't know quite who you were, but I didn't think you were Fancy Nancy."

"I certainly didn't think you were Fancy Nancy," said her father.

"It was the dress that did it," said her mother. "I've never seen that dress before."

Fancy Nancy felt pleased. She showed

her mother and father all the sequins on the dress and explained how she'd bought it at the Jumble Sale and smuggled it home. Then she gave a big sleepy yawn.

"That was a good disguise, Fancy Nancy," said her mother. "Why don't you go upstairs now and put Elizabeth Louella's clothes away safely and then come downstairs and have a hot drink in the kitchen?"

Fancy Nancy sat at the kitchen table sipping her drink and chatting to her mother about spies, witches, wizards and trolls. And then she said, "You know Mrs Judson next door. Well she hasn't seen the green sparkly dress. I bet if I got dressed up in it and crawled along our hedge while she was busy in her garden and then suddenly popped out – well, I bet I could surprise her!"

"You probably could, Fancy Nancy!" said her mother. "You probably could!"

2

Fancy Nancy and the Play

One morning, while Fancy Nancy was having her breakfast, she noticed something new on the mantelpiece between the clock and the photograph of Smelly Baby at the fair with a sailor's hat on. It was a bright orange envelope. Her mother gave it to Fancy Nancy to open. Inside were three pieces of pink cardboard with numbers and letters printed on them.

"They're tickets," said her mother. "Tickets for the theatre. We're going to see Aunt Sylvie in a play next Friday night."

"I didn't know Aunt Sylvie did plays in theatres. I thought she worked in an office," said Fancy Nancy.

"Well, she doesn't do it all the time," said her mother. "She does it in her spare time. It's a hobby."

"Oh," said Fancy Nancy. "Anyway," she went on, looking pleased, "we'll be going out at night."

"That's right," said her mother. "And we'll get Jenny to come and look after Thomas."

Fancy Nancy looked at the numbers and letters on the tickets. They were D4, D5, and D6.

"Which one is mine?" asked Fancy Nancy.

"You can have D5. Then you'll be sitting between me and Dad."

Fancy Nancy had only seen one play and that was the Nativity play at school and she hadn't seen much of that because she'd been busy being one of the shepherds. That morning in school, Fancy Nancy wrote in her book, "I am going to a play at night." And she drew a picture of herself under the stars and moon and wearing her best red spotty dress.

On Friday night, Fancy Nancy's father came home early from work and made the supper while Jenny the baby-sitter and Fancy Nancy's mother bathed Smelly

Baby and put him to bed. Fancy Nancy changed into her red spotty dress and put on a badge shaped like an elephant.

At the theatre, everybody was crammed around the doors and nobody seemed to want to go and sit down in their seats. They were all crushed up against each other and talking loudly. Then a bell rang three times and they all pushed in through the doors into the theatre. Fancy Nancy held on tight to her pink ticket with D5 printed on it and then gave it to a lady in a smart white blouse and black skirt. "Thank you, dear," she said to Fancy Nancy, who noticed that she had black patterns like leaves on the backs of her stockings.

Fancy Nancy had to squeeze past one or two bumpy knees to get to her seat which was rather a rickety wooden chair. She settled down and looked at the big gold curtain hanging across the stage. Every so often something would go bump behind it and a lump or two lumps would make a big bulge in the cloth. Then, one by one, the lights began to go down in the

theatre until there was just one bright light
shining on the curtain.

Fancy Nancy began to feel excited.

"Is Aunt Sylvie behind the curtain?"
she asked her father.

"Yes. Sssh now. The play's going to start," said her father.

Then, slowly, the curtain divided in the middle, slowly pulled back, and Fancy Nancy could see the stage.

It didn't look like the stage at school. It seemed to be turned into somebody's living room. A real living room with doors, chairs, a big sofa, little tables and a lamp, a carpet on the floor, photographs and pictures on the wall and a door that opened out into a garden with a bright blue sky above.

Someone seemed to be trying to get through one of the doors. There was quite a lot of shaking and rattling and then a beautiful woman in a pink dress and a pink hat came through the door and into the living room.

"It's Aunt Sylvie! It's Aunt Sylvie!" said Fancy Nancy.

"Yes, dear. Ssssh!" said her mother.

Aunt Sylvie walked around the living room saying, "Albert! Albert! Albert!" over and over again and screwing her hankie up into a little ball.

Fancy Nancy didn't know what to make of it.

"Where's Albert?" she whispered to her mother.

"I don't know. We'll have to wait and see," whispered her mother back.

Aunt Sylvie sat down on the sofa and cried.

Then lots of people came onto the stage and talked loudly to each other and to Aunt Sylvie. In the play her name was Belinda. They all sounded cross and one man stamped his foot and said he wasn't going to put up with Belinda much longer. Aunt Sylvie started crying again. Fancy Nancy looked at her father and mother. They both looked very serious and sad.

But Fancy Nancy didn't feel sad. She felt a giggle creep up into her shoulders and even though she crossed her arms across her chest and took deep breaths the giggle didn't quite go away. Everybody left the stage to go and play tennis and Aunt Sylvie said she was going to go and have a rest. When the stage was empty, a man came in through the doors from the garden. He had a bunch of flowers in his hand and he took down a photograph from the wall and hugged it tight. And then he said, very sadly, "Oh Belinda! Oh Belinda! I love you Belinda!" This time Fancy Nancy couldn't stop the giggle. The more she tried, the worse it got. Huge, chuckly giggles came one after the other, and the more the man said, "Oh Belinda! Oh Belinda! I love you Belinda!" the more the giggles swelled, popped and exploded.

"Sssh!" said the people sitting in front of Fancy Nancy.

"Sssh! Sssh!" said the people sitting behind.

And "Sssh! Sssh! Sssh!" said Fancy Nancy's mother and father.

Fancy Nancy tried to hush but as the play went on, more and more peculiar things happened. Aunt Sylvie did a dance with Albert and they both bent their knees to the floor and dived and swooped like two seagulls. Then a man in a brown suit and black boots burst into the room and said, "I have returned! I have returned!" and everybody covered their eyes with their hands. He dragged Aunt Sylvie away through the door and out into the garden. Then a policeman came and asked everybody a lot of questions. The policeman went out into the garden and came back with the man in the brown suit and black boots who was snarling dreadfully. The more he snarled and growled, the more Fancy Nancy had to fight to keep the giggles down.

Fancy Nancy thought it might help if she stopped looking at the play altogether. So she turned her head away from the stage and looked along the rows at all the other people watching the play. Everybody was staring at the stage, their sad and serious faces lit by the bright lights. That is to say, everybody was staring seriously except one person. And that person had her handkerchief stuffed in her mouth, her hands clapped over her ears and her knees jammed up to her chin. Fancy Nancy looked and looked again. And then she stared.

"Jumping Jellybeans!" said Fancy Nancy. "That's Jane Dobson from my class at school!"

Fancy Nancy felt a bit better now that she knew Jane Dobson was giggling too, and anyway it looked as if the play was going to be over soon. Aunt Sylvie and Albert kissed each other a lot and so did everybody else, the gold curtains came together again and the play was finished. All the actors came out in front of the curtain and bowed while everybody clapped. Fancy Nancy clapped loudest of all because she was so pleased the play was over and she could stop giggling. Her chest ached and her face was wet with tears.

As she was coming out of the theatre she saw Jane Dobson's mother stop Jane and tidy her hair and straighten her dress. She seemed to be talking to Jane with quite a serious face. And then Fancy Nancy's father stopped *her* and mopped her face with his hankie. "What a giggler!" he said sadly. "What a terrible, terrible gaggling giggler!"

On Monday at school, Fancy Nancy was busy measuring some water into blue mugs and beakers when Jane Dobson came and stood beside her.

Fancy Nancy looked at Jane and smiled.

Jane looked at Fancy Nancy and smiled.

Jane said, "Oh, Belinda! I lerrv you! I lerrv you!"

Fancy Nancy and Jane exploded into giggle after giggle after giggle.

Jane and Fancy Nancy stayed close to each other for the rest of the day. Sometimes they giggled together and Mrs Sims had to tell them to shush. But sometimes they just chattered to each other. They sat next to each other in the book corner at story time, they played together in the playground and they sat next to each other at dinner time. When it was time to go home, Fancy Nancy said she would bring something to school tomorrow for Jane. It was a picture of an exploding volcano that came from a magazine. Jane said that she had an American dollar bill that Fancy Nancy could borrow for a while if she liked.

Fancy Nancy had told Jane all about Smelly Baby so when she saw her mother and Smelly Baby waiting in the playground, she took Jane to meet him. Smelly Baby was eating a big yellow pear and his face was covered in juice and scraps of pear skin. He dropped his pear when he saw

Jane and put his arms up to Fancy Nancy which meant he wanted a hug.

"You see what I mean?" said Fancy Nancy to Jane. "He's not a nice clean sweet baby. He's a horrible old *Smelly* Baby!" And Fancy Nancy bent down over the push-chair and hugged Smelly Baby tight. Jane laughed and said she must run and find her mother.

Fancy Nancy ran after her, "Hey Jane!" she called.

Jane turned back and Fancy Nancy caught up with her.

"Jane," said Fancy Nancy. "Listen! I lerrv you, Belinda! I lerrv you!"

"I lerrv you! I lerrv you, Belinda!" said Jane. As they collapsed into giggles again their mothers came across the playground to hurry them up.

"Come *on*, Fancy Nancy," said her mother.

"Do hurry up, Jane!" said *her* mother.

"OK," said Fancy Nancy, trying to stop giggling. "See you tomorow, Jane!"

"See you tomorrow, Fancy Nancy!" said Jane.

3
Fancy Nancy and the Dog in the Library

One Saturday morning, Fancy Nancy and Jane and some other children were sitting on a stripy red bean bag on the floor of the library. Richard, the librarian, was telling them a story about a tiger who came for tea and ate everything in the house. It was a very good story and Fancy Nancy, Jane and all the other children were listening hard.

Suddenly, out of the corner of her eye, Fancy Nancy saw something move behind one of the bookshelves. It was big and creamy white. It looked like the new carpet at home but it was moving. Fancy Nancy forgot about the story of the tiger and stared. Then she saw that the creamy white shape had legs, a tail, a brown nose, big brown eyes and soft floppy ears.

"It's a DOG!" Fancy Nancy whispered.

"What-are-you-doing-in-the-library-dog?" whispered Fancy Nancy, moving her lips around the words but not speaking aloud.

"Did you say you've got a big green frog?" whispered Jane back.

"No! Look! There's a dog!" whispered Fancy Nancy.

"Oh! He's looking straight at you!" said Jane.

Fancy Nancy spoke out loud. "I can see you, dog. And you're not supposed to be in here because there's a notice on the door that says, NO DOGS!"

"What did you say Fancy Nancy?" asked Richard. "Something about a dog? There're no dogs in this story – only greedy tigers!"

"Look Richard! Look everybody! Look over there!" said Fancy Nancy. "There's a big white dog over there by those bookshelves!"

Everybody looked and everybody shouted, "There's a DOG! A DOG! A big white dog in the library! LOOK!"

Fancy Nancy and Jane climbed off the bean bag and rushed towards the dog. The dog watched them coming and waited. He didn't move until they had almost reached him and then he got up and raced around the corner of the shelves.

"Oooh! Aaah!" shouted Fancy Nancy and Jane.

"Oooh! Aaah!" shouted all the other children.

Then the dog raced on towards another

shelf and ran around that. Then he raced back to the first one. Then he raced backwards and forwards and backwards and forwards. Then he ran round in circles for a while. Then he jumped over the stripy red bean bag and ran round and round Richard's chair. He raced to the desk where all the books were stamped, and knocked over a whole box of library tickets.

"Oooh! Aaaah!" shouted Fancy Nancy and Jane.

"Ooooh! Aaah!" shouted all the children.

All the time the dog was racing around the library, he had a wicked look in his eye and he panted loudly. He knocked big books off shelves. He raced into the grown-ups' library where he pushed his nose against a big board covered with photographs and pictures. It crashed down and just missed his tail. Then he ran into the room where the librarians made their tea. Everybody could hear cups and saucers crashing down and when he came out again he had a whole packet of ginger biscuits in his mouth. He raced back to the children's library and flopped down on the

stripy red bean bag. "Jumping Jig-saws!"
said Fancy Nancy. "He's going to eat the
biscuits!"

And he did! He didn't bother to take
the wrapping off. He just munched and
crunched through the whole packet and
bits of paper and cellophane were spat out
all over the stripy red bean bag.

"Uggh!" said Fancy Nancy and Jane.

"Uggh! Uggh! Uggh!" said all the children.

Fancy Nancy stared hard at the dog. She noticed that he had wicked eyes. But he had a laughing mouth and that might mean that he was friendly. On the other hand he was very big. But then, although he was naughty he seemed to *know* he was naughty. Fancy Nancy was sure of that.

"Come here, dog!" Fancy Nancy said firmly.

The dog took no notice. He went on spitting out pieces of paper and cellophane.

"All right!" said Fancy Nancy, "I'll come to you!" And she marched across the floor to the dog.

"Be careful, Fancy Nancy!" said Jane.

"Oooh! Aaah! Fancy Nancy's going to talk to the dog!" whispered all the children.

Fancy Nancy looked at the dog's big brown eyes and slowly put her hand out and patted his head. It was soft and warm, so she patted some more. Then the big dog rolled over and showed his creamy white tummy. Fancy Nancy stroked and scratched his fur a little. He liked that. Jane came over to join Fancy Nancy and she tickled the big creamy white dog under his chin and he rolled over and over on the stripy red bean bag.

"Look!" said Jane, "Look at his collar, Fancy Nancy!"

Fancy Nancy looked. It was a very complicated dog collar made of leather and twisted into curly, swirly shapes. Dangling from the collar was a round circle of brass with something written on it.

"Jumping Jumpers!" said Fancy Nancy. "That's fancy!" And she and Jane patted the dog's tummy some more. Then all the other children came over to the dog and soon everybody was patting and scratching and stroking and talking to him.

Richard looked at the little brass circle dangling from the dog's fancy collar. "It says his name's Skipper and his phone number is 378901"

"Let's ring up his family!" said Fancy Nancy.

"And tell them Skipper is here and we're looking after him!" said Jane.

So Richard left Skipper with the children while he rang up the number on Skipper's collar. When he came back he said that the family were very happy that Skipper had been found but sorry that he'd been a nuisance.

Skipper sat on the stripy red bean bag with Fancy Nancy and Jane and all the other children. Richard went on with the story of the tiger who came to tea and everybody listened. Skipper put his head in

Fancy Nancy's lap and went to sleep. Fancy Nancy liked the feeling of a big, heavy, warm dog sleeping on her knees, so she didn't move him – even though she could hardly move herself.

When Skipper's family came into the library to collect him he leapt off the bean bag. Everybody thought he was going to start charging around again and steal some more biscuits. But he didn't. He went up to his family, wagging his tail and laughing, and he looked so pleased and happy that Fancy Nancy didn't mind him going off with his family and leaving everybody behind.

When Fancy Nancy's mother came to collect her with Smelly Baby, she heard all about Skipper and how naughty he'd been, but how soft and warm and friendly as well.

"Do you think," said Fancy Nancy as they walked home from the library, "do you think that one day *we* might have a dog like Skipper?"

"We'll see," said her mother. "We'll see."

4

Fancy Nancy, Aunt Belle and the Stepladder

It was Saturday afternoon, and Fancy Nancy was all ready to go and play at Jane's house while her mother and father went shopping for a new carpet, when the phone rang.

"It's Jane's mother. . ." whispered Fancy Nancy's mother. Fancy Nancy came and stood by the phone to try and hear what was going on.

"Jane's got a bad cold. . ." whispered her mother.

"Bother!" said Fancy Nancy. She could hear her mother saying, "Oh dear! Oh dear!" and then, "All right then! Why not!"

Fancy Nancy's mother said, "Would *you* like to talk to Jane on the phone to cheer her up a bit?"

"Hello, Jane," said Fancy Nancy quite loudly. She was not sure about phones.

"Mmmnhello? Hello, Fandy Dandy," said Jane.

"Hello, Jane. It shounds as if you've got a flannel pushed over your nose!"

"I've got a cold in the dose. Dot a flannel over by dose!"

"Listen to this joke. What did one wall say to the other wall?"

"I don't dow. What did one wall say to the odder wall?"

"Meet you at the corner!"

"Oh! I get it! Beet you at the corner!"

"Have you got stuff rubbed on your chest?"

"Yes . . . it sbells yucky!"

"I had stuff on my chest. And it all came off on my nightie."

"I'm dot wearing a dightie. I've got pyjabas on. Dey've got boons and stars all over them."

"Moons and stars!" said Fancy Nancy. "That's fancy!"

Fancy Nancy's mother said it was time to stop talking now so Fancy Nancy said, "Mum says it's time to say goodbye. So I'll see you on Monday at school."

"See you on Bunday. At school if I'm better. Bye-bye."

"I hope she is better on Monday at school," said Fancy Nancy.

"*Now* what shall we do?" said Fancy Nancy's mother. "I know you don't like shopping with me and Dad on Saturday afternoons with Thomas."

That was true, thought Fancy Nancy. She didn't like the way the shops were always so full and noisy and she didn't like shopping with Smelly Baby. He took things off counters and put them in his mouth and once he got out of his push-chair and rolled a tin of paint along the shop floor until it hit a poor man in the ankles. Fancy Nancy had felt very shy and hot when the man shouted at her mother and father.

Now Fancy Nancy had another aunt besides Aunt Sylvie. She was called Aunt Belle. And she was a big aunt. She wore big shoes, she wore big hats and she had a big laugh. Sometimes Fancy Nancy would visit her for tea.

"Why can't I go and see Aunt Belle?" she asked her mother.

"That's a good idea – if she's at home and would like to have you," said her mother, and she telephoned Aunt Belle straight away. Aunt Belle said she'd be very pleased to see Fancy Nancy and could do with her help. So her mother and father dropped her off at Aunt Belle's house and went off shopping for the new carpet with Smelly Baby.

Aunt Belle was painting her kitchen and she gave Fancy Nancy a paintbrush and a small pot of paint and asked her if she'd like to start work on the undercoating for the skirting boards. She covered Fancy Nancy in an old shirt and said it didn't matter about splodges on the wall because the new kitchen tiles would soon cover them up.

Fancy Nancy started painting as carefully as she could. But sometimes the paint was sticky and sometimes it was runny and thin. Fancy Nancy couldn't get it to cover the skirting board without little white islands popping up here and there all over the wall. But Aunt Belle didn't mind.

"Just slap it on Fancy Nancy! That's the ticket!" she called down loudly from the top of the stepladder and she began singing in a big cheerful voice –

"The sun has got his hat on
Hip-hip--hip-hooray!
The sun has got his hat on
And he's coming out to play!"

Suddenly there was a terrible crash!
"YEOW!" yelled Aunt Belle, in a huge loud roar.

"Jumping Jazz Bands!" yelled Fancy Nancy.

For there was Aunt Belle stuck fast in the stepladder. The little platform that she had been standing on had broken away completely and she was standing on the floor, with one side of the stepladder in front of her and the other behind her – and there was paint everywhere.

"Help!" roared Aunt Belle. "Help me, Fancy Nancy! I'm stuck!"

Fancy Nancy was thunderstruck. She walked slowly round the stepladder which was wrapped round her big aunt and tried to think of a plan. Aunt Belle was too big to pull out of the top, past the broken platform, and she was too big to squeeze

49

through the sides. What was to be done?

"Try wriggling a bit," said Fancy Nancy. Aunt Belle wriggled as best she could but there wasn't much room to move – let alone wriggle.

"Or try a big jump," said Fancy Nancy. "Maybe you can jump out."

"I don't think I'll try *jumping*," said Aunt Belle firmly.

"I know!" said Fancy Nancy. "Why don't you try and lie down and sort of wriggle your shoulders and your legs and you might come out of the end of the ladder?"

"It's worth a try," said Aunt Belle.

Fancy Nancy held the sides of the stepladder carefully. Aunt Belle slowly lowered herself to the floor.

"Now what?" said Aunt Belle breathlessly, "Now what do I do, Fancy Nancy?"

"Well . . . you sort of wriggle and push yourself along the floor at the same time," said Fancy Nancy. "And I'll hold the sides of the ladder steady so that you can squeeze through."

So Aunt Belle wriggled a little and

pushed a little and Fancy Nancy held onto the ladder until, with one last wriggle and with one last push, Aunt Belle was free, and Fancy Nancy helped her get up from the floor.

Aunt Belle huffed and puffed and gave a big laugh. "Blow this painting nonsense, Fancy Nancy! Let's get cleaned up, go out and buy a new stepladder and come back here for a big tea!"

Fancy Nancy noticed a big creamy white dog tied up outside the hardware shop. "Now there's a decent sized dog," said Aunt Belle and gave him a big pat on the head.

"That's Skipper!" said Fancy Nancy. "That's Skipper, Aunt Belle. He ran away once and escaped into the library. He ate up all the ginger biscuits! Hello, Skipper!" Fancy Nancy gave Skipper a few strokes under his soft chin.

Skipper wagged his tail.

Inside the shop were ladders and lawnmowers, buckets and brooms, string, coils of wire, pots and pots of paint and rows of paintbrushes. While Aunt Belle was buying the new stepladder, Fancy Nancy was looking at a box on the counter. Inside the box were tiny pots of paint of different colours and the pots were no bigger than cotton reels.

"Doing a bit of painting, love?" asked the lady behind the counter, seeing that Fancy Nancy's hands were still covered in white splodges of paint.

"Yes," said Fancy Nancy. "Sort of."

And she asked, "How much are the little pots of paint?"

"Oh they're free today," said the lady. "They're samples. You take the little pot home and try it out and if you like the colour you come back to the shop and buy a big pot."

"Mmmn!" said Fancy Nancy, thinking hard of the things she could paint with a little pot of paint.

"Would you like one?" said the lady. "Go on! Choose yourself a nice bright colour!"

Fancy Nancy looked hard at the little pot of bright orange paint. "That's the colour I'd like. That orange colour please."

"That's right, dear! Choose something cheerful!" said the lady and she put the little orange pot of paint in a bag for Fancy Nancy.

Fancy Nancy helped Aunt Belle to carry the new stepladder out to the car. Skipper was still there and he thumped his tail on the pavement when Aunt Belle and Fancy Nancy went by. When they got to

Aunt Belle's house, she said she'd had enough of painting for one day and would Fancy Nancy like to butter the buns for tea. When Fancy Nancy's mother and father arrived to take her home, Aunt Belle told them all about the broken stepladder and how Fancy Nancy had rescued her.

Fancy Nancy showed everyone her little pot of orange paint.

That evening, before supper, Fancy Nancy asked her father if there was anything she could paint to make a present for Jane.

"There's your old wooden egg cup. That's got no paint left on it now," he said.

"An orange egg cup!" said Fancy Nancy. "That's fancy!"

Her father spread some newspaper over the kitchen table and found a little brush. Fancy Nancy carefully painted the egg cup a lovely glowing orange and put it on the mantelpiece to dry.

On Monday morning, the orange paint on the egg cup was dry, bright and shiny. Fancy Nancy wrapped it up in a scrap of red tissue paper and took it to school to give to Jane, even though she didn't know for sure that Jane's bad cold would be better. But there was Jane waiting for her in the playground. Fancy Nancy held the parcel of tissue tightly in her hand and stuck out both her fists in front of Jane.

"Go on," said Fancy Nancy. "Choose which hand's got a surprise in it! Close your eyes!"

Jane shut her eyes and touched one of Fancy Nancy's fists. "That one! That's the one with the surprise!" said Jane.

And she was right. It was.

5

Fancy Nancy and the Bad Quarrel

Fancy Nancy woke up one morning in a bad mood. She couldn't find her rainbow socks, and her jeans with the red patches on the knees were in the wash. That made her bad mood worse. At breakfast she spilled the cornflakes and her mother said, "Clear that up, Fancy Nancy," in a cross voice. She saw something interesting about dinosaurs on the back of the cornflakes packet and showed her father. He said he didn't have time for that now and would she please hurry up with her breakfast. Then Smelly Baby dropped one of his big wooden blocks in the milk jug and the milk splashed all over Fancy Nancy's dress. Fancy Nancy wanted to change her dress but her mother told her not to fuss and mopped up the milk with a tissue.

"But when it dries, it will stink of smelly milk!" said Fancy Nancy, crossly.

"No it won't," said her mother.

"It will! It will! It WILL!" shouted Fancy Nancy.

The night before, Fancy Nancy had found some good pictures of ants eating their way through a tree in the jungle. She had cut them out of the magazine carefully and was going to take them to school to show Mrs Sims, her teacher. Now she was rummaging around the living room trying to find an envelope to put them in. Her mother was busy getting herself and Smelly Baby ready for the walk to school. Every so often she called to Fancy Nancy, "There's an old brown envelope in the waste-paper basket. Use that and hurry up!"

Fancy Nancy didn't want the old brown envelope. Someone had put a chewed apple core on top of it and now there was a dark wet splodge right in the middle of it. So she was looking through the desk and trying to find a clean white envelope and all the bills and letters were scattered over the floor. When Fancy Nancy's mother

came into the living room and saw the mess she was not best pleased.

"Fancy Nancy! Put all those things back in the desk! And HURRY UP!" said her mother angrily. "And you can just use that old envelope in the wastepaper basket!" Fancy Nancy's mother marched across the room, took the envelope out of the waste-paper, dusted it off on her coat, took Fancy Nancy's ant pictures and put them briskly inside.

"But that envelope's got horrible brown muck on it!" wailed Fancy Nancy.

"Never mind. It will do," said her mother and they set off for school.

When Fancy Nancy got to school the first thing she saw was her friend Jane showing her stickers to a girl called Leila. They were both laughing. "I bet they're laughing at *me*," thought Fancy Nancy and she felt even crosser. She stomped into the cloakroom to hang up her coat and put the brown envelope on the floor underneath her coat peg. A boy called Roger Cummings came over to look at it.

"What's in it?" he asked Fancy Nancy.

"Pictures of ants," said Fancy Nancy.

"You've been sick all over it. That brown mark is your sick. Ugh!"

"It is *not*!" said Fancy Nancy.

"You have. Uggh! Uggh! Fancy Nancy's been sick all over an envelope for Mrs Sims!"

"You stop saying that, Roger Cummings!" said Fancy Nancy in a very angry voice. And she hit Roger as hard as she could on the arm.

Roger stamped on Fancy Nancy's toes.

Fancy Nancy wailed and Mrs Sims came running into the cloakroom.

"Now then! Now then! What's the matter?" said Mrs Sims.

"He stamped on my toes," said Fancy Nancy.

"She hit me on the arm!" said Roger.

"Say 'Sorry', Fancy Nancy," said Mrs Sims.

"Sorry," muttered Fancy Nancy. She didn't feel sorry at all.

"Say 'Sorry', Roger," said Mrs Sims.

"Sorry, Fancy Nancy," said Roger, and he didn't feel very sorry either.

Mrs Sims said they had both better come and help her get the classroom ready.

Mrs Sims said she liked the pictures of

the ants when Fancy Nancy showed them to her. She said she would show them to the whole class before they started work that morning. But she didn't. Leila hurt her finger in the playground and Mrs Sims had to take her to the staff room to get a plaster. By the time she came back she must have forgotten about the ants because everybody got straight on with their work. That made Fancy Nancy even crosser.

Jane came and helped Fancy Nancy get out the blocks and bricks for number. She asked Fancy Nancy why she was looking so cross and sad.

"Because I am cross and sad," snapped Fancy Nancy.

"I expect you got out of the wrong side of the bed," said Jane.

"I've only got *ONE* side of the bed to get out of, silly! I've got bunk beds! SILLY!"

"All right! All right!" said Jane, and went off to ask Leila if her finger was better.

Fancy Nancy was working on her number when Roger Cummings came up and stood behind her. Fancy Nancy knew he was there.

"Go away – BADGER! Go away Roger! You big fat badger!" said Fancy Nancy quite loudly.

"I was only coming to look. . ." said Roger.

"GO A-WAY!" said Fancy Nancy and she settled down to her number and drew three beautiful red and blue flowers. But then she went over to Roger and stood behind him while he was working on a puzzle. She picked away at a bit of loose wool on his jersey.

"GO AWAY, FANCY NANCY!" shouted Roger.

Jane saw what happened. "Can't you just stay out of his way today, Fancy Nancy?" she said kindly.

"He's in *my* way," growled Fancy Nancy. "He should stay out of *my* way!"

"Seems to me you're *both* in each other's way!" said Jane. "Would you like to borrow my stickers for the rest of the day?"

"I don't want any old stupid sticky stickers!" snarled Fancy Nancy, and stormed off to the book corner to find the book about volcanoes. Somebody else was reading it. So Fancy Nancy went off to the workroom where Roger Cummings was making a clay pot. As Fancy Nancy went past, she put her finger – SPLAT – right in the middle of it.

At dinner time, Roger whispered, "Sick! Sick! Sick!" as Fancy Nancy was standing in the line waiting for her turn. At story time, Fancy Nancy poked Roger hard on the leg with a wooden brick.

Mrs Sims tried every way she could to stop Roger and Fancy Nancy quarrelling, but in the end she had to ask Fancy Nancy to stay next to her for the rest of the afternoon and do puzzles or look at a book. Fancy Nancy was furious. She wanted to paint a picture of the ants. When it was time to go home, Jane said they could ask their mothers if Fancy Nancy could go home with Jane and stay for supper. But by this time Fancy Nancy was so upset and miserable that all she wanted to do was to go home and be by herself.

Fancy Nancy's mother could tell at

once that Fancy Nancy was miserable. Her shoulders were hunched and she was looking down at the ground with a fierce cross face.

"Have you had a bad day, Fancy Nancy?" she asked.

"I've had a horrible day!" said Fancy Nancy, and she burst into tears.

Her mother bent down and cuddled her and that made Fancy Nancy cry some more. She told her mother all about the bad quarrel with Roger. She told her how he'd been horrible about the envelope and how he'd stamped on her toes. She told about Mrs Sims forgetting to show everyone the ant pictures. After a while, she told her about hitting Roger, poking him in the leg and teasing him and how she'd had to stay with Mrs Sims and not do any painting. Then she cried some more. Smelly Baby leaned out of his push-chair and grabbed Fancy Nancy's coat and cuddled it to his cheek. He did not like to see Fancy Nancy cry. Fancy Nancy began to feel a little better.

All the time that Fancy Nancy was telling *her* mother about *her* horrible day, Roger Cummings was telling *his* mother about *his* horrible day. He told his mother about Fancy Nancy teasing and hitting him and he also told her about how he'd been nasty about the brown mark on the envelope. And after he'd had a good cry he felt better too.

On the way home Fancy Nancy's mother stopped at the greengrocer's to buy some potatoes. When Fancy Nancy walked into the shop the first person she saw was Roger Cummings buying apples with his mother. Fancy Nancy noticed that Roger's eyes were red and watery but she didn't stare at him.

Roger's mother took the bag of apples from the greengrocer and was just going to put it in her basket when the bag broke and all the bright red apples scattered over the floor.

Fancy Nancy dived for the biggest red apple!

Roger dived for the same apple!

Crash! Their heads banged together!

They both sat back on their heels, rubbed their heads and then began to smile. Then they both laughed and picked up the rest of the apples together.

When it was time to go, Fancy Nancy said, "Goodbye, Roger."

"Goodbye, Fancy Nancy. See you tomorrow," said Roger.

Fancy Nancy's mother made jacket potatoes for supper, and Fancy Nancy had lots of grated cheese on hers. After supper she told her father all about her bad day but it didn't seem quite so bad now. She didn't feel angry with Roger any more and

she could ask Mrs Sims to show everybody the ant pictures tomorrow. She settled down on the sofa with her father to listen to her story. It was very exciting. It was all about a troll with green toes who tried to capture a princess but she was too clever for him and he ended up in the bottom of the deepest well in the whole world.

"I'll be able to paint a picture of that in school tomorrow," said Fancy Nancy, and she climbed into her warm bunk bed and went fast asleep.

6

Fancy Nancy and Jane and the Wild Animals

One morning, during the Spring half-term holidays, Fancy Nancy and Jane were playing wild animal tamers in Fancy Nancy's living room. Smelly Baby was a

wild lion. Jane was the person who owned him and Fancy Nancy was the Amazing Maree – the world famous lion tamer. Fancy Nancy had made Smelly Baby a cage out of cushions from the sofa and she had a string of tea-towels tied together which she was using to tame him with. When they were all ready, Jane came out into the middle of the living room and said, "Ladies and Gentlemen! May I present Leo! The worst woman-eating lion in the whole world and his tamer – the Amazing Maree!"

As Smelly Baby crawled and roared around the living room, Fancy Nancy waved the tea-towels and shouted in a very loud voice, "Down! Down! Down! Leo! Down!" and "Back in your cage, Leo! Back! Back! Back!"

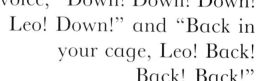

And then, the Amazing Maree laid a string of tea-towels across the floor and shouted, "Jump! Leo! Leo, Jump!"

Smelly Baby crawled over the tea-towels.

"And now," said Jane, "the Amazing Maree will reward him!"

"For what?" asked Fancy Nancy.

"For jumping," said Jane. "For doing his tricks!"

"Oh," said Fancy Nancy. "Well here you are, Smelly Baby. I mean Leo. Here's a leg of giraffe for you! Eat it up!" And Fancy Nancy handed Smelly Baby an old copy of the Radio Times and pushed it towards his mouth. Smelly Baby spat it out.

Fancy Nancy's mother came into the living room and said it was time for Thomas's rest and she took him off to his cot to sleep. Fancy Nancy and Jane went out into the garden with the string of tea-towels to see if there was anything out there in the way of wild animals they could tame. It was a bright blue and yellow day. The sun was gleaming but there was a cold wind blowing across the garden. Fancy Nancy and Jane shivered a bit. They went to look inside the hole that Fancy Nancy had been digging for a long time. It was coming along, getting bigger and bigger and muckier and muckier. They saw two snails crawling through the soil.

"I bet we could tame them," said Jane, and she made a little bridge out of sticks for the snails to crawl over.

Fancy Nancy flapped the tea-towels.

"Snails!" she shouted. "Cross the bridge! At once! Now!"

When the snails came to the bridge they stopped. Very slowly they put out their horns and touched the sticks. Very slowly, they turned around and crawled the other way.

"Oh, look!" said Jane. "They're still wild snails. They're not tame at all."

Fancy Nancy watched the snails crawling slowly back towards the big hole.

"Look!" said Fancy Nancy. "There're two worms coming out of the hole!"

"They're going fast!" said Jane. "I bet they're having a race!"

"I bet the dark brown one gets to my shoe first!" said Jane.

"I bet the pink slithery one gets to me first!" said Fancy Nancy.

Fancy Nancy flapped the tea-towels. "Faster!" she cried. "Bright pink slithery, slothery wriggly worm! Go faster! Get to me first!"

The two worms slithered and slothered and wriggled and jiggled towards Fancy Nancy and Jane. And then they stopped. Suddenly. And burrowed head down deep into the soil – away and gone. Fancy Nancy and Jane watched them go.

"Oh!" said Fancy Nancy.

"They don't seem to want to be tamed either," said Jane. "What about those birds over there by the washing line? They might sit up on our shoulders if we tamed them."

They both rushed towards the birds, and Fancy Nancy flapped the tea-towels in the cold wind.

"Birds! Birds!" she cried. "Fly up on our shoulders! At once! Now!" But the birds flew away over the gardens and trees.

As they were standing by the washing line Fancy Nancy thought she heard a strange noise coming from the garden next door. It was a sort of mewing, yowling noise and it seemed to come from Mrs Judson's shed. Mrs Judson was a very tidy lady and she had a very tidy garden. There were no big holes and not much washing – only a few tea-towels and they went back inside after a very short while. She was quite a kind lady but she was a bit fierce. She had very black eyebrows and grey hair.

Fancy Nancy said, "I can hear a noise from Mrs Judson's shed. It's a sort of yowling. Listen."

They both listened.

Jane said, "I bet that's a wild animal!"

Fancy Nancy said, "It could be Mrs Judson – trapped by a wild animal!"

Jane said, "We'd better go and look."

They both carefully climbed over the fence.

Mrs Judson's garden was very quiet. Fancy Nancy and Jane peered towards her house where they could see her kitchen

window but there was no sign of her. Then the yowling began again. Fancy Nancy held the tea-towels tight as tight. Fancy Nancy and Jane began to go towards the door of the garden shed.

"Do you think it's a very big animal?" asked Jane.

"No – if it was big and had got Mrs Judson round the leg we would hear her yelling for help," said Fancy Nancy.

"But the yowling might *be* Mrs Judson," said Jane.

"Mmmn!" said Fancy Nancy and she

flapped her tea-towels a little bit. "You open the door and I'll sort of push it with my foot at the same time."

The door opened. There was a big hiss and a huge yowl and a black shape went whizzing past their ankles.

"Yeow!" yelled Fancy Nancy.

"Yeow!" yelled Jane. The black shape whizzed round the flower beds and all around the lawn and then it scrabbled and whizzed up Mrs Judson's plum tree where it sat on a branch and looked cross.

"It's that cat!" said Fancy Nancy. "It's that cat that lives down the road and sits on the wall outside! Its name is Bumble."

Fancy Nancy put her tea-towels down on the lawn and went and stood under the branch and looked up at Bumble.

"Maybe we could tame him down from the tree," said Jane, and she picked up Fancy Nancy's tea-towels and gave them to her. Fancy Nancy flapped the tea-towels hard and knocked the heads off a few snowdrops. Jane jumped up and down on some crocuses and clapped her hands together smartly.

"Be still, Bumble!" shouted Jane.

"Be quiet and peaceful, Bumble!" shouted Fancy Nancy.

Bumble hissed and yowled.

"And just what do you think you two are up to?" said a loud voice.

Mrs Judson! It was Mrs Judson looking as cross as Bumble and twice as fierce.

"Fancy Nancy!" said Mrs Judson, "Did you do *this*?" And she pointed to the broken snowdrops. "And did you do this as well?"

she said, pointing to the broken crocuses.

Fancy Nancy looked at Jane. Jane looked at Fancy Nancy. Then they both looked at their feet.

"I broke the crocuses. I was trying to tame Bumble," whispered Jane.

"And I was trying to tame Bumble too. And I broke the snowdrops," whispered Fancy Nancy. Jane and Fancy Nancy looked at the broken flowers.

"And what are all these tea-towels doing here?" asked Mrs Judson, looking even crosser.

"They're for taming wild animals," said Fancy Nancy.

"You won't get far with them! Tea-towels!" snapped Mrs Judson.

Fancy Nancy tried to make the crocuses stand up straight again.

"I'm sorry, Mrs Judson," said Fancy Nancy.

"And I'm sorry too, Mrs Judson," said Jane.

"Well it's no good crying over broken crocuses," said Mrs Judson, briskly. "What are we going to do about this poor cat?"

"I don't know," said Fancy Nancy, whose face had been getting redder and redder and more and more miserable.

"Come on! Cheer up both of you! Come and help me find some food for Bumble! See if we can tempt him down out of the tree!" said Mrs Judson.

Fancy Nancy and Jane followed Mrs Judson into her house. They helped her mash up some left-over fish fingers and poured some milk into a saucer. Then they carried Bumble's food carefully back to the plum tree.

"Now I think it would be a good idea if we went back into the house and had a snack ourselves. And I'll ring up Bumble's owner."

Fancy Nancy and Jane sat on Mrs Judson's sofa in her living room and munched a handful of raisins and drank some orange juice. Outside in the garden, Bumble climbed down the tree, and started to eat the food. Mrs Judson was speaking on the telephone. Fancy Nancy and Jane tried hard to listen.

"Oh it wasn't *me* who found Bumble,"

said Mrs Judson. "It was Fancy Nancy and Jane!"

Fancy Nancy and Jane looked pleased.

Soon Bumble's owner came to fetch him home. Fancy Nancy and Jane gave him a stroke and said goodbye. He was not a yowling, hissing black shape any more, just an ordinary friendly cat.

Mrs Judson said it was time for Jane and Fancy Nancy to go home now and would they mind going home by the front door, and not over the back fence, please.

Fancy Nancy picked up her tea-towels.

"I'm sorry about the broken flowers," she said, as she and Jane went out of Mrs Judson's front door.

"There, there! No harm done! Well, not much, anyway," said Mrs Judson, giving them both a cheerful push.

When Fancy Nancy and Jane were having their lunch, they told Fancy Nancy's mother all about Bumble and the broken flowers.

"Oh dear!" said Fancy Nancy's mother. "Mrs Judson will be sad. She loves her flowers."

"I know what we'll do!" said Fancy
Nancy. "We'll make her a garden!"

And they both set to work. They found
an old pie dish and filled it with soil. Then
they got some interesting looking weeds
and planted them round the edge. They
cut up some yellow material and some blue
material and made flower shapes to stick
in the earth. Fancy Nancy found a little
mirror to put in the middle of the garden to
make a pond. Jane made a swan out of
plasticine to swim on the pond. You could
see the swan's reflection beautifully in the
shiny glass. When it was all ready they
asked if they could knock on Mrs Judson's

front door and leave the garden on her doorstep as a surprise.

They walked up Mrs Judson's front path very carefully and quietly. They put the garden on the step, rang the doorbell loudly and then raced home again as fast as their legs could carry them. Just as they were going to go through their front door they heard Mrs Judson open her front door.

"Good heavens!" said Mrs Judson. "A pie plate garden! What a lovely surprise!"

7
Fancy Nancy's Birthday

It was Fancy Nancy's sixth birthday and everybody was settled around the breakfast table, waiting for her to open her presents and cards. Smelly Baby held onto the parcel he was supposed to give Fancy Nancy. He didn't want to let go of it because the paper had pictures of elephants all over it and it was good to chew as well.

"Don't chew my present up, Smelly Baby!" said Fancy Nancy.

Smelly Baby chuckled and handed over the rather damp parcel.

Fancy Nancy opened the present carefully. Inside was a smart red torch and four batteries.

"Jumping Jig-saws!" said Fancy Nancy. "That's just what I need to search for trolls and wild animals!" Fancy Nancy's mother fitted the batteries into the torch and Fancy Nancy clicked the switch on and looked under the table. It was very interesting. She saw lots of lumps of toast that Smelly Baby had dropped on the floor, she saw the little green plastic horse that had come out of the cornflakes packet and one of her rainbow socks that she'd been hunting for.

"Thank you, Smelly Baby," said Fancy Nancy, and she gave him a hug. Smelly Baby gave her a wet kiss on her nose.

Fancy Nancy opened her next present. It was a long flat shape and it came from Aunt Belle and there was a card to go with it with a picture of a stepladder and a pot of paint. Aunt Belle had written "Paint the Town Red on your Birthday!" Inside the parcel was a box of paints that were all the colours of the rainbow and had names like cobalt blue, indigo, violet and crimson.

"They look like pretty fancy paints," said Fancy Nancy happily.

Aunt Sylvie's present was a book. It was called "Make Your Own Play" and it showed how to make scenery, how to make costumes and how to put on make-up and it had some interesting ideas for stories that could be made into plays. Fancy Nancy started to read one of them. It was all about a clever queen who built a bridge across a waterfall which was full of poisonous snakes.

"Get a move on, Fancy Nancy," said her father. "I know it's a good story but it's nearly time to go to school and you've still got one more present to open."

Fancy Nancy opened her last present.

It was from her mother and father and it was a bright blue T-shirt with red whales printed all over it.

"Oh, thank you!" said Fancy Nancy, although she felt puzzled. A bright blue T-shirt with whales printed all over it was nice, but it was only a T-shirt. Then her father said, "It doesn't seem much of a present, does it, Fancy Nancy?"

"Well it does – sort of," said Fancy Nancy.

"Don't worry," said her mother. "You've got another present coming later on. A very special present. We're going to collect it in the car after school and Jane can come with you."

"Is it a very big present?" asked Fancy Nancy, making a big circle in the air with her arms.

"No. It's not big like that," said her father. "In fact, at the moment it's quite small. It's about *this* size." And he made a shape with his hands that was about as big as the cornflakes packet.

"Mmmmn!" said Fancy Nancy. "At the moment. . ."

Jane was waiting for Fancy Nancy in the playground at school, with Fancy Nancy's birthday present held tightly in one hand and her birthday card in the other.

"Open it carefully!" she said to Fancy Nancy. "And Happy Birthday!"

Fancy Nancy unwrapped the first layer of red paper. Underneath the red paper there was a layer of newspaper and lots of sticky tape and underneath the newspaper there was brown shiny paper and more sticky tape and underneath the brown shiny paper there was yellow tissue paper and more and more sticky tape.

Fancy Nancy started to giggle.

"This is a pretty fancy parcel!" she said, and unwrapped the last of the paper and tape. And there was the present. It was a bright purple china mug with FANCY NANCY printed in gold letters around the middle.

"And that's a *very* fancy mug!" said Fancy Nancy. "Thank you!"

Fancy Nancy showed her present to Mrs Sims, who said she would keep the mug in a safe place until it was time to go home.

There were two other children who had birthdays on the same day as Fancy Nancy, and in Assembly that morning they all came out in front of the children and teachers. Mrs Sims played the piano and everybody sang "Happy Birthday." Then Mrs MacGregor, one of the dinner ladies, brought in three sponge cakes with six candles on each of them, all burning brightly. Fancy Nancy blew out her candles in one puff and took her cake back to the classroom, where Mrs Sims helped her to cut it up into pieces for everybody to have a taste and a wish. Fancy Nancy made her wish very quietly to herself. She was thinking about the special present that was still to come. The present that was about as big as the cornflakes packet "at the moment. . ."

The day at school went very slowly. Fancy Nancy kept asking Mrs Sims what to do next. She tidied up the book corner and she sorted out the dressing-up box. She

stared out of the window when she was supposed to be writing a story about frogs. Then she half painted a picture of frogs but gave up doing that because the legs looked like elephant's legs. At last it was home time and Fancy Nancy and Jane raced to get their coats. Fancy Nancy held on to her purple mug carefully and showed it to her mother.

Fancy Nancy, Jane and Smelly Baby all squeezed into the back of the car. Fancy Nancy's mother turned the car around and drove away from the school and down a road that Fancy Nancy had never seen before. They passed a football ground

and a big bus station. They went over two bridges, and then they seemed to travel for ages down a road that had trees on one side and a railway line on the other. Fancy Nancy could not think where on earth a special present could be on a railway line. Then they stopped outside a house with a blue door.

"Is this where the present is? But it's somebody's house! I thought it would be in a shop!" said Fancy Nancy, as she climbed out of the car.

A lady opened the blue door, and standing beside her was a big golden-coloured dog that wagged its tail and put its nose into Fancy Nancy's hand. The lady said the dog's name was Bess.

"Hello, Bess!" said Fancy Nancy, looking all around her for her special present and patting Bess's warm head at the same time.

The lady smiled. "Your present is in the kitchen, Fancy Nancy. Come and have a look!"

"Maybe it's something to eat," thought Fancy Nancy, and followed the lady into the kitchen. It was just an ordinary kitchen and there didn't seem to be anything special to eat. In fact there didn't seem to be anything special at all. And then she saw the puppy.

There, on the floor by the boiler, was an old brown blanket which had been torn and chewed to shreds. In the middle of the blanket, snoozing with its head on its paws, was a soft, sleek golden puppy.

"Oh! Oh!" said Fancy Nancy.

"The puppy is your special present, Fancy Nancy," said her mother.

"Oh! Oh! Oh!" said Fancy Nancy. She felt hot and pink and shy. She crouched down on the floor beside the puppy and patted its head softly. It opened one eye and looked at her.

"Pick him up, Fancy Nancy," said the lady. Fancy Nancy picked the puppy up carefully. He was soft and warm and floppy. He put his nose into Fancy Nancy's collar and snuffled and sniffed.

"Oh! Oh! Oh!" said Fancy Nancy and gave the puppy to Jane to hold for a little while. The puppy wriggled a little.

"I think he likes you best," said Jane and she gave the puppy a cuddle and gave him back to Fancy Nancy. Fancy Nancy put the puppy back on the blanket and Smelly Baby crawled over to have a look. He lay on the puppy's blanket and stared inside the puppy's ears. Then he patted the puppy's wet nose and tried to curl up beside him and go to sleep. The lady told Fancy Nancy that the big dog Bess was the puppy's mother. She told her that her puppy was a male dog and that she'd have to think of a good name for him. She said that he still needed a lot of looking after, because he was only six weeks old.

"Oh I'll look after him! I'll look after him!" said Fancy Nancy.

The puppy didn't like the car much. He sat on Fancy Nancy's knee, and although she hugged him when loud buses went past or when they went round sharp corners, he whimpered and cried. And then, just after they'd gone round one very sharp corner, he was sick all over Fancy Nancy. Jane helped Fancy Nancy clear the mess up with tissues.

"Yuk!" said Fancy Nancy. "What a stink!"

"Never mind," said her mother. "We'll be home soon, and do you remember when you used to be sick in the car when you were little?"

"Only sometimes," said Fancy Nancy but she cuddled the puppy some more and whispered, "Home soon . . . home soon."

When the puppy got home the first thing he did was to make a big puddle in the kitchen all over the floor. Jane kept Smelly Baby out of the way while Fancy Nancy and her mother mopped it all up.

"I used to make puddles sometimes when I was little, didn't I Mum?" said Fancy Nancy as she squeezed out the mop.

"Sometimes," said her mother, and then she showed Fancy Nancy all the things for the puppy that she had hidden away, and that the puppy would need. There were two bowls – one for water and one for food. There was a brush and comb for grooming, there was a big plastic tray full of newspaper for the puddles and there was a wicker basket for him to sleep in. They had brought his old chewed blanket with them so that he would have something comfortable and familiar to sleep on. Fancy Nancy took the blanket and made the puppy a soft bed inside the basket but he didn't seem to want to sleep, so Jane and Fancy Nancy took him all over the house and showed him everything. He liked the bathroom best. He knocked over the dirty washing basket and began chewing a couple of vests.

Fancy Nancy took a few days to decide on the best name for her puppy. In the end she decided to call him Jones.

Jones kept everybody very busy. He needed a lot of feeding with special meals – four times a day at first. Fancy Nancy emptied his tray and kept his water bowl full and tried to keep him out of trouble. He chewed one of Smelly Baby's slippers and Fancy Nancy's father's best tie. One day, Fancy Nancy's mother left the shopping on the floor and he took all the potatoes and hid them under the living room sofa, and he didn't always use his tray. He still made puddles sometimes. But as the weeks went by, Jones grew bigger and stronger, and he was allowed out for walks. Fancy Nancy's father took him for a good long run every day, but every morning Jones walked to school with Fancy Nancy and her mother and Smelly Baby, and every afternoon he was waiting for her in the playground.

Jones was always pleased to see her and he was always in a good mood. Fancy Nancy knew that even if she was in the worst mood possible and had had the most miserable day ever, if she had just had an ordinary day or if she had had the most wonderful day, Jones would always greet her in the same way. He would run round her three times with his tail wagging and push and shove his wet friendly nose into her hand. Then he would sit upright and hold out his paw to her, as if she were the best friend he had in the whole wide world.